First published in this format in 2015 by Curious Fox,
an imprint of Captsone Global Library Limited,
7 Pilgrim Street, London, EC4V 6LB
– Registered company number: 6695582

www.curious-fox.com

CAPG35035

Originated by Capstone Global Library Ltd
Printed and bound in China.

ISBN 978 1 78202 306 7
19 18 17 16 15
10 9 8 7 6 5 4 3 2 1

A full catalogue record for this book is available
from the British Library.

Curious Fox

THE MYSTERY INC. GANG!

SCOOBY-DOO

SKILLS: Loyal; super snout
BIO: This happy-go-lucky hound avoids scary situations at all costs, but he'll do anything for a Scooby Snack!

SHAGGY ROGERS

SKILLS: Lucky; healthy appetite
BIO: This laid-back dude would rather look for grub than search for clues, but he usually finds both!

FRED JONES, JR

SKILLS: Athletic; charming
BIO: The leader and oldest member of the gang. He's a good sport – and good at sport, too!

DAPHNE BLAKE

SKILLS: Brains; beauty
BIO: As a sixteen-year-old fashion queen, Daphne solves her mysteries in style.

VELMA DINKLEY

SKILLS: Clever; highly intelligent
BIO: Although she's the youngest member of Mystery Inc., Velma's an old pro at catching crooks.

When an archaeologist shares her discoveries about the legend of Atlantis, Mystery Inc. gets wrapped up in a dangerous curse. Only **YOU** can help the gang solve this legendary mystery!

Follow the directions at the bottom of each page. The choices **YOU** make will change the outcome of the story. After you finish one path, go back and read the others for more **Scooby-Doo** adventures!

YOU CHOOSE the path to solve the mystery of...

The Mystery Inc. gang is excited to be in Bimini, a small island in the Bahamas that's connected to the legend of Atlantis. "Dr Jackson said she'd meet us at the airport," Daphne says.

BEEP! BEEP! Their archaeologist friend drives up in a Jeep that looks as though it's held together with chewing gum and duct tape.

"Hi, gang! Welcome to Atlantis!" Dr Danielle Jackson exclaims as the gang climb into the Jeep.

"Zoinks! We're in Atlantis? Like, I thought we were in the Bahamas," Shaggy says.

"Well, the theory is that these islands are all that's left of the sunken continent," Dr Jackson replies.

Turn the page.

"Ratlantis sank?" Scooby-Doo moans.

"Like, are we safe?" adds Shaggy.

"Don't worry, that was thousands of years ago," Dr Jackson says. "Most people don't believe Atlantis existed, but I've found a clue that it did!"

"The mystery of Atlantis is the greatest in history, and we love a good mystery!" Fred says.

"This one even comes with a curse!" Dr Jackson laughs.

"A ... a curse?" Shaggy and Scooby gulp.

"Fishermen and divers are thought to have gone mad or gone missing. I'm sure it's all just made up by the locals," Danielle says.

"You don't believe in the curse, but you believe in Atlantis?" Velma points out.

"When it comes to Atlantis, I have proof," Dr Jackson replies. She drives the gang to her research ship. It's a rickety diving boat that has even more duct tape on it than the Jeep.

"Ruh-roh," Scooby says with a sinking feeling.

Dr Jackson and the gang board the boat and sail out to very deep, dark water.

"Rat rooks spooky," Scooby says.

"The water is very dark here because we're over a sea cliff,' Jackson explains. "Let's take the plunge!"

The gang gets into scuba gear and jumps into the water. Danielle guides them down the face of the underwater cliff.

"Stop!" Dr Jackson shouts to Mystery Inc. through their helmet radios. "Now, turn around and look..."

The gang sees a giant carved statue of a human with the head of a dog. "That's Anubis, the Egyptian god of the dead!" Velma says. "Why is an Egyptian statue here in the Bahamas?"

"Because of Atlantis. But there's more," Dr Jackson replies. She swims into the mouth of the statue. Mystery Inc. follows Dr Jackson into a large chamber. They turn on their underwater diving lamps and gasp at what they see.

Turn the page.

The walls are painted with images of ancient royalty.

"These pictures look like a mixture of Egyptian and Mayan art. That's odd," Velma observes.

"That's Atlantean," Dr Jackson announces.

While Velma and Dr Jackson discuss the paintings, Shaggy and Scooby see something sparkle in the shadows. Shaggy points his diving light at it and sees a giant eyeball!

"*Yaaa!* A sea monster!" Shaggy shrieks. He churns his legs in the water and zooms backwards. Shaggy hugs Scooby for comfort.

The gang shine their lights on the object. It's actually a crystal ball in the wall.

"That wasn't here before," Jackson says. "The currents must have washed away the silt."

"It looks like pure crystal," Velma observes.

"It looks Atlantean," Danielle Jackson declares.

None of them can resist touching it.

The crystal ball glows, getting brighter and brighter. Suddenly a ghostly figure jumps out of the crystal! It looks human and wears a crown of coral on its head. Its mouth moves, but no one can hear what it's saying.

"I've seen him somewhere before," Fred says.

"He's in one of the paintings," Dr Jackson realizes and points to a picture on the wall. "It's the king!"

"Zoinks! He's come back to haunt us! This place is cursed!" Shaggy moans.

"I think he's trying to warn us," Daphne says. "Look how he's waving his arms."

Suddenly a swirling vortex forms around them. It gets stronger and stronger.

"Hang on! Don't split up!" Fred shouts over the helmet radio.

It's too late. They spin away from each other in different directions, into the unknown darkness.

To follow Shaggy and Scooby, turn to page 12.

To follow Fred and Velma, turn to page 14.

To follow Daphne and Dr Jackson, turn to page 16.

Scooby and Shaggy cling to each other as they get swirled around and around by the underwater vortex. Soon they are very dizzy! They don't know if they're upside down or sideways!

"Zoinks! I feel like we're stuck in a washing machine set on the spin cycle!" Shaggy moans.

A second later they feel like they are being sucked up by a vacuum cleaner. Shaggy and Scooby are pulled through a hole in the wall by an even stronger current. The current pulls them into a tunnel.

"Ruh-roh," Scooby cries as the current carries them deeper.

The strong rush of water sends Shaggy and Scooby through the tight, twisty tunnel. The friends hold onto each other and tumble like a ball down a chute. *THUMP! WHUMP!* Shaggy bumps up against the narrow wall. *RIIIP!* His scuba helmet comes off his head!

"BLUUURP!" Shaggy shouts before he remembers to hold his breath!

"Rim, Raggy! Rim!" Scooby encourages his friend.

Shaggy puts his hand on Scooby's collar, and the friends start to swim along with the current as fast as they can. They can't see anything in the dark tunnel. Shaggy starts to turn red, then blue. He has no more breath.

"Blooby-Doooo," Shaggy whimpers with his last gasp.

WHOOOOOSH! Suddenly Shaggy and Scooby are flying through the air. Their arms and legs spin, but they aren't swimming. They're in a geyser!

The friends fall out of the fountain of water and onto dry land. Shaggy gasps for breath. A second later he gasps in fright. A tribe of fierce natives scowls at the unexpected visitors.

"Ruh-roh," Scooby says. "Run!"

If Shaggy and Scooby escape, turn to page 18.

If the tribe captures the twosome, turn to page 25.

Fred holds on to Velma but can't grab any of his other friends. Velma grabs Fred, but the rest of the diving team spins away from her in the vortex. The water twirls them around and around like an underwater tornado.

After a while the vortex slows down and dissolves. Fred and Velma drop out of it and float in calm water. They are very dizzy.

"Wh-where are we?" Velma wonders.

"I don't know, but wherever it is, it sure is dark," Fred replies. He turns on his diving lamp and tries to look around.

"We aren't in the Anubis temple anymore," Velma realizes when she turns on her diving lamp and sees that they are in a cave.

"We must have been caught in an underwater current and carried here," Fred decides.

"Can you see a way out?" Velma asks. "We need to get back to the surface."

Fred and Velma swing their diving lamps around, but all they can see are the walls of the cave.

"I can't see a way out," Fred replies.

"So how did we get in?" Velma wonders.

Suddenly a long, shadowy shape swims around the two friends.

"Jinkies! What was that?" Velma yelps in surprise.

"I think it was a giant eel," Fred replies, unsure.

"*Yaaa!* It's got me!" Velma yells. The shape swims off into the dark holding Velma captive.

Fred catches a glimpse of the creature as it swims through a gap in the cave wall. He doesn't know why he and Velma didn't see the opening before. He doesn't care. Velma is in danger! Fred follows as fast as he can.

Fred doesn't go very far. He stops on the other side of the gap and is amazed by what he sees!

If Fred finds a secret lab, turn to page 20.

If Fred thinks he sees mermaids, turn to page 27.

The strong underwater vortex spins Daphne away from her friends. She sees a shape in the swirling water and reaches out to grab it. "I've got you!" Daphne says as she grabs someone's flipper.

"Daphne! Is that you?" Dr Jackson asks over the helmet radio.

"Dr Jackson, can you see any of the others?" Daphne asks.

The vortex kicks up silt and mud from the ancient temple and creates a blinding cloud. "I can't see anyone except you," says Dr Jackson.

Daphne and Dr Jackson have no control and bump into the temple wall. **THUMP! THUMP! CRASH!** The last hit is so hard that part of the wall collapses.

"Jeepers!" Daphne exclaims as she falls through the opening.

Daphne doesn't let go of Dr Jackson's flipper, and they both tumble out of the vortex and into a small chamber. The chamber is full of glittering objects.

"Are those diamonds, Dr Jackson?" Daphne asks.

"Please call me Danielle, and no, it's better!" Danielle exclaims. "Those are crystal skulls!"

"*Ewww!*" Daphne exclaims when she sees the eerie objects. "They're spooky-looking."

"They're from Atlantis!" Danielle proclaims. "They're supposed to have mystical powers. This is a great discovery!"

Daphne shines her diving light on the skulls. Suddenly they start to glow. One of the skulls shoots out two beams of light, one from each eye socket. The beams strike two other skulls. A third beam forms a triangle with Daphne and Danielle in the middle.

"Is that supposed to happen?" Daphne asks.

"I have no idea," Danielle admits.

Suddenly the water begins to shimmer. So do Daphne and Danielle. Their bodies start to tingle.

"Uh-oh. This can't be good," Daphne realizes.

If they enter a portal to Atlantis, turn to page 23.

If the skulls give them a strange history lesson, turn to page 29.

Shaggy forgets that he only just avoided drowning and that he was propelled onto dry land by an underground geyser. There's a tribe of natives in front of him with fierce frowns painted on their faces – they are holding big pointy sticks.

"Run!" Scooby shouts. Shaggy doesn't argue.

The friends speed away from the geyser and the terrifying tribe. They race into the jungle and don't look back.

But Shaggy and Scooby don't get very far. The island is very small. They emerge from the jungle and onto the other side of the island in just a few minutes.

"There's no escape, Scoobs!" Shaggy moans.

Suddenly Scooby sticks his tail out straight, and his nose points at something in the distance. It's a boat anchored just off shore.

"You did it, Scoob! We're saved!" Shaggy exclaims.

Shaggy and Scooby stand on the beach and wave at the boat. They jump up and down to catch the attention of the people on board.

"That's got to be Dr Jackson's boat," Shaggy says. "Like, who else would be out here?"

Shaggy and Scooby are happy to see a small motor boat speed towards the shore. They are not happy to see that the people on the boat are dressed in black diving suits and are holding weapons!

"Zoinks! That's not Dr Jackson," Shaggy gulps.

Shaggy and Scooby turn to run back into the jungle to hide. As soon as they do, they see the natives standing at the edge of the forest.

"Re're doomed," Scooby sighs.

If Shaggy and Scooby are captured by the natives, turn to page 32.

If Shaggy and Scooby get caught by the armed divers, turn to page 48.

Fred suddenly stops chasing the creature that has Velma. He is so astonished at what he sees that he can't help himself. He is in a large cave with lots of light. He sees that the cave is equipped like a science lab. Then he sees that a giant, mutant eel has Velma wrapped in its coils!

"Well, I was right about the eel," Fred says as he rushes towards the creature.

The eel swims into a large hollow in the cave wall. It settles down into a nest of loose rocks but does not unwrap its body to release Velma. The eel closes its eyes and seems to go to sleep.

"Oh, great, it's going to have a nap before it eats Velma," Fred groans.

"Get me out of here, Fred," Velma screams over the helmet radio. She squirms against the eel's body but can't break free.

Turn to page 22.

Fred looks around for a way to release Velma from the giant mutant eel. He notices that the lab equipment looks like something out of a science fiction film. The equipment is sleek and shiny, but nothing is made out of metal.

"Wow, this is super high-tech," Fred says as he pauses to admire the designs. "Everything is made out of plastic. Hmm, that makes sense if it's under water. It won't rust."

"Fred! A little help, here!" Velma shouts.

"Sorry, Velma!" Fred replies. He grabs an object that looks like a broomstick. It isn't made of wood. Fred doesn't know what it is or what it's made out of, but he thinks he can use it to pry Velma out of the eel's coils.

Fred swims up to the sleeping eel. He is about to free Velma when the mutant creature begins to wake up!

If Fred battles the mutant eel, turn to page 34.

If someone grabs Fred before he can help Velma, turn to page 52.

The shimmering water slowly fades around Daphne and Danielle. Suddenly, they are on an ancient wooden ship, being thrown around on rough seas! They hang on to each other to stay on their feet. That is when they realize they aren't in their diving suits anymore. They are dressed in strange clothing. It appears they've gone back in time.

BOOOOOM! An enormous explosion draws their attention towards the stern. They can see three volcanoes erupting. The blast creates a tidal wave that is heading directly towards the ship.

"Captain! Turn the ship to follow the wave! We can ride it away from the shore!" someone shouts. Daphne realizes that it's her voice. She has no idea how she knows this information.

The captain stares at her as though she's crazy, then shrugs and turns the rudder. The ship catches the tsunami and rises up onto the wave like a surfboard.

Turn the page.

The ship is lifted higher and higher and suddenly starts to move with the wave. The passengers scream but hang on. They are about to get the ride of their lives.

The ship rides the tsunami. It carries them far away from the island. They can't see land, and they can't see any other boats.

"Thank you for saving the ship," the captain says to Daphne. "Atlantis is gone, but at least some of us will survive."

"We've just witnessed the destruction of Atlantis!" Danielle gasps. "My theory was correct!"

"I'm not worried about theories right now," Daphne says. "I'm worried about whether we'll ever see land again."

"That's one of my theories – that survivors of Atlantis made it to Europe and Egypt and started the civilizations there," Dr Jackson says.

"You and I will witness that, too, unless we can find a way back home," Daphne worries.

If they find land, turn to page 36.
If they face danger at sea, turn to page 55.

Shaggy and Scooby-Doo try to run away from the fierce natives, but their flippers get in the way. *FLAP! FLAP! FLAP!* They waddle like big ducks. The native warriors quickly catch up with them.

"Zoinks! We're doomed!" Shaggy wails. Scooby whimpers and hugs his pal.

The warriors tie up the twosome with a thick rope. Then they secure Scooby and Shaggy to a large pole. The pole is lifted by several of the natives and carried on the natives' shoulders.

Shaggy and Scooby are taken through the jungle to a small village. In the middle of the village is a large fire pit with a giant iron pot resting on smouldering coals. Something is simmering in the pot. Scooby's nose twitches.

"*SNIFF! SNIFF!* Rat smells good!" Scooby says.

"Oh, no! I think we're going to be dinner." Shaggy moans.

Turn the page.

Thankfully, Shaggy and Scooby are carried past the pot, but they soon face something even scarier. The tribal king comes out of a huge hut and scowls at the captives. Shaggy and Scooby gulp at the fierce frown on his face, and he isn't wearing any face paint!

The Queen follows the King. Her face shows no emotion. She stares straight ahead. Shaggy and Scooby recognize her!

"V-Velma?" Shaggy stammers.

She doesn't answer her friends.

"Intruders! You have invaded my kingdom!" the king says to Shaggy and Scooby-Doo. "You will face the punishment – the cooking pot or combat. You choose!"

Shaggy and Scooby look at each other and gulp.

"Like, either way, we're doomed," Shaggy groans.

If **Shaggy and Scooby go into the cooking pot**, turn to page **68.**

If **the friends end up in combat**, turn to page **86.**

Fred swims into an underwater chamber and is startled by what he sees. The chamber is bright with light. The good thing is that now he can see the creature that has captured Velma. The bad thing is that he can see the creature that has captured Velma!

At first Fred thinks his eyes are playing tricks on him because of a lack of oxygen. It's a mermaid that has Velma, and not just one. The chamber is full of the legendary creatures.

"Am I dreaming? Is this real?" Fred wonders.

Velma's voice on his helmet radio assures him that this is real.

"Fred! I could use some help!" Velma shouts.

"Well, I guess I was wrong about the eel," Fred decides and swims towards his friend.

A group of mermaids blocks Fred from the mermaid holding Velma. They wear armour made from sea shells and point coral spears at him.

Turn the page.

"Wait! I come in peace!" Fred says and holds up his hands.

The mermaids squeal like dolphins. One of them pokes Fred with her spear.

"Ow!" Fred yelps.

The mermaids look at each other and chatter in a high-pitched language. Another mermaid pokes him. Fred yelps again. The mermaids smile at his reaction. They like the sound he makes! The whole group points their spears at him.

"I'm not a squeaky toy!" Fred proclaims.

SHREEEEE! Suddenly an ear-shocking sound stops the mermaids. They back away from Fred and Velma.

The queen of the mermaids swims towards Fred, Velma and her subjects. She is as large as an orca and looks twice as fierce.

"We're doomed," Fred and Velma gulp.

If the queen claims Fred and Velma as her property, turn to page 71.

If the queen declares Fred and Velma are enemies, turn to page 89.

The triangle of light from the crystal skulls makes the water shimmer around Daphne and Dr Jackson. It forms a pyramid over them! Images move across the three glowing sides.

"Look! It's like a projection screen for a film," Daphne exclaims. She is more curious than afraid.

"This isn't a film, Daphne, it's the crystal skulls!" Dr Jackson exclaims. "The images are coming from inside them."

Daphne and Dr Jackson watch in wonder as a parade of scenes shines across the walls of water.

"Those are the ancient Mayans! That's Egypt before the pyramids!" Danielle shouts over the diving helmet. "This is the greatest discovery of my career!"

"What's this?" Daphne asks. She points to images of a disaster. The wall of water displays scenes of tidal waves and erupting volcanoes.

"I-I think that's the destruction of Atlantis," Dr Jackson whispers in awe.

Turn the page.

Daphne and Dr Jackson float in the underwater chamber. They are surrounded by incredible images.

"I think these are recordings from the past," Dr Jackson says. "The crystal skulls are like library books."

"Then we need a librarian," Daphne says. "Hello! Is there a librarian in the house?"

Suddenly Daphne hears Scooby-Doo's voice!

"Relp! Relp! Ri'm *dooooomed*!" Scooby wails.

Daphne and Danielle see two images of Scooby-Doo in two different walls of water. One shows Scooby as a pup. The other shows Scooby in Egyptian clothing.

"Scooby is in danger! I have to help him!" Daphne exclaims.

"We don't know if these are just recordings or portals to the past!" Dr Jackson warns. "Besides, how do you know which Scooby to choose?"

If Daphne chooses to save the Scooby pup, turn to page 73.
If Daphne chooses to help Egyptian Scooby, turn to page 93.

"Like, we're stuck between a tribe of angry natives and bad guys in black," Shaggy says.

"Rhat way?" Scooby asks.

ZAAAP! ZAAAP! Energy bolts shoot past them from the bad guys on the motor boat. Shaggy and Scooby throw themselves onto the ground and cover their heads with their hands. The natives rush towards them. They want to reach Scooby and Shaggy before the men in the boat do.

The natives win the race. They grab Shaggy and Scooby and carry the twosome into the jungle. The friends are so afraid that they shut their eyes and expect the worst to happen. They are surprised when they hear a voice proclaim:

"Honoured Ones! Welcome to the Fountain of Youth!"

Shaggy and Scooby slowly open their eyes. They aren't in the jungle anymore. They are in a cave. The walls are covered with barnacles and crusty coral. The natives bow to Shaggy and Scooby.

"Honoured Ones! We are the guardians of the Fountain of Youth. You came up out of the magic water. We are here to serve you!" the leader declares.

"Serve us?" Shaggy repeats. He and Scooby look at each other and think the same thing. *Food!*

A little while later, Shaggy and Scooby sit in front of a banquet. There are piles of baked oysters and mounds of cooked fish. A giant pot of seafood stew simmers over a fire, and a mountain of tropical fruit reaches to the top of the cave.

"You know, I like being an Honoured One!" Shaggy says with his mouth full of food.

Turn to page 38.

"Uh-oh," Fred gulps as the giant mutant eel opens its eyes and stares straight at him.

"Fred, I think we're in trouble," Velma shouts over the helmet radio.

"Oh, we're in trouble all right!" Fred replies. He churns his flippers in the water to get away as the mutant eel snaps at him.

"There are eggs in here," Velma says. "This is a nest. The eel isn't a monster, it's a mummy!"

Velma wiggles out of the creature's coils and swims over to Fred. She wraps her arms around Fred and hugs him as hard as she can.

"Velma! I-I didn't know you felt this way about me," Fred stammers.

"I don't! Now hug me or we're doomed!" Velma says.

Fred and Velma hold on to each other as tight as possible. The giant eel glares at them with its giant eyes. Then it seems to understand.

"The eel wasn't trying to squeeze me, it was trying to hug me," Velma explains. "It was like a handshake."

"That was some handshake!" Fred declares.

"I wanted to show it that you and I were friends, too, by hugging you," Velma says. She reaches out and pats the mutant eel on the head. It accepts the friendly gesture and goes back to its nest for a nap.

"I'm glad we've made a new friend, but we have to find a way out of here before our air runs out," Fred says.

Suddenly a swarm of divers swims into the cave. They are dressed in black diving suits and surround Velma and Fred.

"I'd suggest a hug, but they don't look very friendly," Fred observes.

Turn to page 42.

The ship carries Daphne, Danielle and the survivors of Atlantis across a muddy sea. There is no wind, so the ship drifts.

"When Atlantis sank it must have churned up the sea and wrecked the weather patterns," Danielle observes. "This information is going into my next book!"

"I hope we get home again so you can write that book," Daphne replies.

"Land!" the captain shouts and points at the horizon.

The current finally carries the ship onto a beach littered with splintered trees and rocks and wreckage.

"It looks like a hurricane hit here," Daphne says.

"This is where the tidal wave hit the shore," Danielle says sadly. "This stuff is all that's left of Atlantis."

"We will start anew from the ruins of the old!" the captain proclaims.

"Then it's time to meet your new neighbours," Daphne says and points at a tribe of cavemen. "Neanderthals!"

The tribe moves cautiously towards the ship as though it's a dangerous monster. They point their stone-tipped spears at it but don't come too close.

"We have to show them that we're friendly. We need a peace offering," Daphne says.

She looks around the ship for something that would send a universal message.

"Food!" Daphne realizes. "Get ready for a prehistoric Scooby Snack!"

Daphne grabs some pickled fish and a loaf of bread from the disaster rations. She grabs one of everything from the emergency supplies to make a giant sandwich.

"Scooby-Doo would love this. I hope you do, too," Daphne says as she climbs off the ship and offers the sandwich to the tribe.

Turn to page 45.

"Rhis is paradise." Scooby sighs as he gobbles down a pawful of seafood.

"It can be this way forever," the leader says.

"I sure hope so. The food here is fantastic," Shaggy declares.

"Your wish is granted," the leader declares. "The Honoured One called Shaggy will stay with us until the end of time."

"Wait. What?" Shaggy sputters. "Like, I can't stay. It's nice that you saved us from those men in black, but we have to get back to our friends. They might be in danger from the bad guys."

"Reah!" Scooby agrees.

"You have eaten the food of the Fountain of Youth and made the wish to stay. Now you can never leave!" the leader shouts.

"Zoinks! That's the curse!" Shaggy realizes. "People come here and never leave! Now we know why!"

"No, it's not a curse, it's a wish," the tribal leader says.

"A wish? Like Aladdin?" Shaggy wonders.

"Who is Aladdin?" the leader asks.

"You know, the guy with the magic lamp? He found it in the desert?" Shaggy tries to explain.

"What's a desert?" the leader asks. "Oh, never mind! You have made the wish. You and the dog must remain here forever."

"Ri'm not a dog, Ri'm Scooby-Doo!" Scooby declares. He grabs Shaggy's diving suit in his teeth and runs.

The natives chase Scooby down a dark tunnel. Suddenly he bursts into another underground chamber. He and Shaggy are surprised to see their friends there!

"Fred! Daphne! Velma!" Shaggy shouts. They are tied up and sitting on crates of seafood.

The tribal leader and the rest of the tribe rush into the cave.

"I knew you kids were trouble." The leader wipes off the face paint. Mystery Inc. recognizes the woman under the disguise.

Turn the page.

"Dr Jackson?" the gang gasps.

"No, my evil twin, Diane!" the real Dr Jackson exclaims. She enters the cave, followed by the men from the motor boat. They grab her twin. "Thanks for helping me expose her seafood smuggling ring!"

"I would have gotten away with it, too, except for that kid and his weird dog," Diane grumbles. "They ate all the sleeping sauce on the seafood I fed them, but they didn't fall asleep."

"She's the one who made up the curse about people disappearing," Dr Jackson says.

"If anyone came here, I pretended to be a guardian of the Fountain of Youth and imprisoned the intruders in these caves," Diane confesses.

"Too bad you didn't know the tummy power of Shaggy and Scooby-Doo!" Velma declares.

THE END

To follow another path, turn to page 11.

The divers grab Fred and Velma and drag them through a steel doorway. The door shuts and is sealed, and then the water drains from the small chamber.

"This is an air lock." Velma sighs with relief.

When all the water has gone, a second door opens. Fred and Velma are shoved into a dry lab and meet the man in charge.

"You meddling kids," the man growls. "How did you find my secret underwater lab?"

"That's your lab? It's great!" Fred says as he takes off his diving helmet. "Except for the giant mutant eel."

"The eel is one of my genetic experiments," the man says. "Too bad it took over the lab and forced me out."

"Wait a minute. I know you!" Velma exclaims. "You're Dr Eevel. I've read about your genetic experiments. They were declared to be too dangerous."

"What? Dr Evil?" Fred gulps.

"No, no. *Ee-VEHL*. It's a tricky pronunciation," the man tries to explain. "Never mind. You kids have discovered my secret lab, even though I invented the curse to keep people away."

"Well, there isn't a curse that Mystery Inc. can't undo," Fred boasts.

"You kids are clever," Dr Eevel admits. "Maybe you can tell me what to do with you two now that you've discovered my secret."

Before Fred or Velma can answer, the floor and walls shake as thought there is an earthquake. Alarms start blaring. The men in the black diving suits flee from the dry lab.

"The eel is on a rampage!" one of the men shouts as he runs past Dr Eevel.

Suddenly the eel crashes through the wall and into the dry lab. It spots the scientist and hisses at him. Then it lunges towards Fred and Velma!

The giant eel grabs Fred and Velma. The lab starts to flood and the gang quickly put their helmets on.

Turn the page.

"She's trying to rescue us!" Velma exclaims.

The eel carries Velma and Fred to the surface and lets them go. Suddenly they are surrounded by a group of baby eels.

"Her eggs have hatched!" Velma says. "It was time to move her family. I guess she thinks of us as part of her family, too."

"Bye-bye! Thanks!" Fred waves as the giant eel swims away with her babies. "Hey, look! There's our diving boat!"

As Fred and Velma swim towards the boat, they hear a voice.

"Wait for me!" Dr Eevel shouts.

"You're going to jail as soon as we get to land," Fred declares.

"Well, at least I'll be safe from my experiment!" Dr Eevel says. "That eel is one mad mother."

THE END

To follow another path, turn to page 11.

"I hope this sandwich makes Scooby and Shaggy proud, wherever they are," Daphne says. She holds her creation out to the tribe.

SNIFF! SNIFF! One of the Neanderthals catches the scent of the food. He lifts off his feet and floats towards Daphne! **SNIFF! SNIFF!** Another Neanderthal drifts through the air.

"*Mmmmm!*" the two tribesmen sigh. They both reach for the sandwich and grab it at the same time. They start to fight.

"Oh no, now I've started a war," Daphne moans.

ROAAAARRRR! Suddenly an animal roar stops the food fight. The scent of food has attracted a sabre-toothed tiger!

"Daphne! Run!" Danielle shouts from the ship.

"Too late," Daphne gulps as the prehistoric predator skulks towards her.

The Neanderthals forget their fight over the sandwich and grab their spears. They wave the weapons at the tiger but the animal ignores them. It wants Daphne!

Turn the page.

"If I'm going to be a part of Atlantean history, it's not going to be like this," Daphne declares.

Daphne looks around for something to defend herself with and sees a piece of mirror in the tsunami rubble. She grabs it and points it towards the sun.

FLAAAASH! Bright light is reflected into the big cat's eyes. **FLAAAAASH!** The sabre-toothed tiger uses its paw to swipe away the light but can't. Confused and annoyed, it turns on its tail and retreats.

The Neanderthal tribe is impressed and runs up to Daphne. They pat her on the head and shoulders as a sign of approval.

"*Mmmm!*" one of the Neanderthals says and offers Daphne the peace sandwich.

"*Mmmmm!*" Daphne replies and chomps down on her own creation. Her face twists up as her taste buds rebel. Suddenly she feels dizzy and faint.

"How can Shaggy and Scooby eat this stuff?" Daphne mumbles.

"What stuff? Wake up, Daphne! You're dreaming!" Shaggy says.

Daphne opens her eyes and sees all her friends. They are on the deck of the diving boat with Dr Jackson.

"There was a booby trap in the Anubis temple, but Fred disabled it," Danielle explains.

"The trap was the reason why the locals thought there was a curse," Fred says.

"We got caught in it, but we all got out, except for you, Daphne," Velma says. "We couldn't find you and we were so worried. Where were you?"

"In Atlantis," Daphne smiles. "And do I ever have a story for you!"

THE END

To follow another path, turn to page II.

Shaggy and Scooby face two terrifying choices. Do they get caught by the fierce island natives, or do they get caught by the men in the motor boat?

BA-ZAAAT! BA-ZAAAT! The men in the motor boat fire energy blasts at the twosome. The energy blasts miss Shaggy and Scooby but make the natives flee.

"Well, it looks like we don't have to decide which is worse anymore," Shaggy observes as the tribe runs away into the jungle.

The men in the boat surge onto the beach and surround Shaggy and Scooby before the trembling twosome can get away.

"Like, we surrender!" Shaggy says as his knees shake.

Scooby's teeth chatter so much that he can't speak. All he can do is put his paws in the air. The men wrap them up with ropes.

"March!" the commander orders and shoves Shaggy and Scooby towards the jungle.

Shaggy and Scooby march through the thick plants until they come to a campsite. They see several tents and a large mound covered with a tarpaulin. That's all they glimpse before they are shoved into one of the tents. They are surprised at what they see inside!

"Daphne! Velma! Fred! Dr Jackson!" Shaggy exclaims. Their friends are tied up and sitting inside the tent.

"You're not going to get away with this!" Dr Jackson shouts at the men as they leave the tent. She struggles against the ropes holding her.

"Like, who are those guys?" Shaggy asks.

"We don't know, but I'm guessing they're criminals," Velma declares. "I'll bet they made up the curse to keep people away from this island."

"What could be on this little island that would make someone go to such extremes?" Dr Jackson asks.

Turn the page.

"I think we have a mystery on our hands," Fred says.

"And now that we have the whole team here, I think it's time we did some investigating," Daphne declares.

"But, re're all ried up," Scooby whimpers.

"Not for long," Daphne says with a mysterious smile. She starts to wriggle inside the ropes. Suddenly they fall off and drop to the ground. Daphne is free.

"How did you do that?" Fred gasps.

"Oh, it's just a little ninja trick I learnt from my martial arts teacher," Daphne replies.

Daphne unties her friends. They creep over to the tent opening and peek outside. They don't see any guards. There is no one near the tent.

"Where has everyone gone?" Velma wonders.

"Maybe it's the curse!" Shaggy shrieks. "It made everyone on the island disappear!"

Turn to page 58.

Fred doesn't dare move. He's floating right next to the mutant monster, and the giant eel is waking up!

"Fred! Look out!" Velma shouts a warning over the helmet radio.

Suddenly Fred is grabbed from behind and pulled away from the sleepy eel.

"Velma!" Fred yells and reaches out to his friend, but he is being carried away from her.

Fred twists and squirms and tries to escape from whatever has hold of him. He turns around and comes face-to-facemask with something beyond his imagination.

He is in the grip of a creature that is part human and part fish. It has the body of a man, the huge eyes of a deep-water tuna-fish, and the snout of a dolphin. Instead of arms and legs, it has flippers and a tail. Fred glimpses a set of gills on its neck.

"*Yaaa!*" Fred shrieks in surprise.

The fish-man creature lets go of Fred and claps his flippers to his ear holes. Fred sees his chance to escape and spins his flippers as quickly as he can. *THWUMP!* Fred bumps into one of the lab machines.

Velma watches Fred sink to the floor of the lab. She shouts to him over the helmet radio, but Fred is unconscious. The fish-man floats above her friend like a silent ghost.

Velma struggles to break free from the giant eel so she can help Fred. Her movements annoy the creature. It turns its massive head towards Velma and opens wide to show her its mouth full of sharp teeth.

"I'm doomed," Velma gulps.

The fish-man swims up to the eel and tickles it under the chin. The serpent relaxes its coils. Velma swims free.

"Th-thank you," Velma says.

Turn the page.

Velma swims over to Fred.

"Fred! Are you okay?" Velma asks.

"Sure. Just get the number plate of the whale that hit me," Fred mumbles.

The fish-man swims through the water towards Velma and Fred. It is the most graceful motion Velma has ever seen. His body looks like it's made up of awkward parts, but it is perfect for a life under water.

Velma and the fish-man lift Fred and take him from the lab. They swim into a chamber decorated with sculptures and treasures that make Velma gasp.

"I recognize these things from the paintings in the Anubis temple!" Velma realizes. "These are from Atlantis!"

"So am I," the fish-man says.

Turn to page 62.

The refugee ship from Atlantis finally floats on calm waters. But the peace doesn't last.

Suddenly one of the passengers screams! She points at something in the water. The captain rushes over to the rail and looks into the water. So do Daphne and Danielle.

"We're in Dragon Waters! All hands, be alert!" the captain shouts.

Suddenly a shape breaks through the water's surface, then another. People shriek in terror.

"Jeepers! It's just dolphins," Daphne sighs in relief.

"Wait a minute. Did the captain say Dragon Waters?" Danielle asks. "You know, ancient mariners' maps always have a section marked 'Here There Be Dragons'. I wonder if that's what he means."

"Please, Danielle! No more of your theories," Daphne moans.

"It's not a theory anymore! Look!" Danielle says and points out to sea.

Turn the page.

Giant shapes dive in and out of the water and head straight towards the ship.

"Dragons!" the captain shouts. "All hands to defense stations!"

The crew scrambles to follow the captain's orders, but the refugee passengers accidentally get in the way. The experienced crew can't get to their stations in time. **BAWOOOM!** Something hits the ship. Daphne and Danielle are almost knocked off their feet. They hug each other for support.

"Wow! It really is a dragon!" Daphne gasps in awe and fear.

"It's a plesiosaur!" Danielle shouts over the screams of passengers and crew.

The sea beast is the first of many that attack the pod of dolphins around the ship. The whole hull of the ship vibrates as the sea monsters hit it.

"Now I know why they say 'shiver me timbers'!" Danielle exclaims.

Suddenly Daphne hears shrill shrieks from the sky. She looks up and sees a flock of something amazing flying towards the ship. Creatures with wide, leathery wings glide over the sea.

"Incredible..." Daphne gasps.

"Pterosaurs!" Danielle exclaims.

"Aren't they supposed to be extinct?" Daphne asks.

"So is Atlantis..." Danielle murmurs as humans and prehistoric animals collide.

Turn to page 65.

Suddenly Dr Jackson bursts out of the tent and runs across the campsite.

"What's she doing?"

"I don't know!"

"She's doomed!"

Dr Jackson hears her friends, but she ignores their warnings. She's willing to brave any danger. She sees her dream treasure.

Dr Jackson runs to the mound covered with the tarpaulin. She skids to a stop and lifts the corner of the canvas. Glittering gold sparkles in the sun.

"This is from my underwater temple! This is from Atlantis!" Dr Jackson proclaims. "Someone is stealing my artifacts!"

"Do you think it could be art smugglers?" Velma wonders.

"Zoinks! Do you think they could come back?" Shaggy worries.

"Wait a minute. This stuff looks funny," Velma says.

"Shaggy's right. The bad guys could come back. Let's get out of here," Daphne agrees.

"No! This is a clue," Velma says and studies an artifact in her hands. Then she glares at Dr Jackson. "This artifact is a fake!"

"*Whaaat?!*" Dr Jackson gasps.

"There isn't any corrosion or coral growth on this object. It hasn't been under water. It has to be new," Velma declares. "That means the temple is new, too. It's a fake."

"Well, I wouldn't make it up! That would ruin my whole career!" Danielle protests.

"Then the only other explanation is that a rival has set you up," Fred concludes. "Someone wants you to look bad."

"No! I don't want to ruin her, I want to help her!" a voice declares.

Dr Jackson and the gang turn to see a man backed up by the people from the motor boat.

"I care for Danielle," he says. "And I just want to make her wish come true."

Turn the page.

"Sam? Sam Carter?" Dr Jackson gasps when she sees him. "I was trying to prove the existence of Atlantis and you faked it? That isn't helping."

"I'm sorry," Sam replies. "I faked the artifacts, but the temple is real."

"Okay, but what about that ghost with the coral crown?" Shaggy wonders.

"What ghost?" Sam asks.

"I think you still have a mystery on your hands," Fred tells Dr Jackson.

"Yes, the mystery of Atlantis!" Dr Jackson proclaims. "Do you want to help me solve it?"

Shaggy and Scooby look unsure.

"Would you do it for a Scooby Snack?" Dr Jackson asks.

The answer is obvious!

THE END

To follow another path, turn to page 11.

"My name is Panto," the fish-man says. "Who are you, and why have you invaded my home?"

"My name is Velma Dinkley. This is Fred Jones, Jr," Velma replies. "We're pleased to meet you, Mr Panto."

Velma reaches out her hand to shake his flipper. Panto doesn't respond.

"It's okay. This is a gesture of friendship," Velma explains. "I don't know what the custom is ... was ... in Atlantis."

"It was the same in Atlantis, but no one has ever offered to shake hands with me before," Panto says and holds up his flipper.

"Then let me be the first!" Velma declares and grasps his flipper with her fingers.

"Hi, Panto!" Fred says and shakes Panto's flipper, too.

"You aren't like any other humans I've met," Panto says with a tear in one large, tuna eye.

"Wait until you meet Scooby-Doo!" Fred says.

"How long have you lived down here?" Velma asks.

"I don't know. I stopped counting when I ran out of room on the wall," Panto replies. Fred and Velma look at the cave wall and see that it is filled with scratches to mark the days that have passed.

"*Hmm*. According to legend, Atlantis was destroyed more than ten millenniums ago," Velma says. "If you're from Atlantis, that means you're at least ten thousand years old."

"That's a lot of scratch marks on the wall..." Fred whispers in awe.

"I didn't realize it had been so long. I really don't get out much," Panto admits with a shrug.

"Panto! You're ten thousand years old! That's amazing!" Velma says.

"It's a curse!" Panto replies. "Would you want to live that long in a body like this?"

"Your body is perfect! I saw you swim through the water, and it was beautiful!" Velma replies.

Turn the page.

"I frighten humans every time I leave this cave. So I don't leave anymore," Panto sighs sadly.

"You don't frighten me or Fred," Velma points out to Panto. "And I know some other people who would be very happy to meet you."

"Hey! Dr Jackson would be thrilled to talk to a real Atlantean!" Fred exclaims.

"Let us take you to our friends," Velma offers. She reaches out her hand.

"O-okay," Panto agrees and reaches out his flipper. "Can I bring my pet eel?"

THE END

To follow another path, turn to page 11.

The flying giants dive down towards the refugee ship. Daphne is afraid that the creatures are going to attack the humans. She is surprised when the passengers and crew start to cheer!

"Huracan! Huracan!" they shout.

Daphne and Danielle watch the creatures fold their wings against their bodies like giant seagulls and dive into the water.

"They're attacking the plesiosaurs!" Daphne gasps in surprise.

"They must be enemies, or else they're feeding," Danielle observes.

"What are the people calling them? Huracan?" Daphne asks as the passengers cheer.

"Huracan is the Caribbean god of winds. It's where we get the word hurricane," Danielle replies. "I guess the pterosaurs are gods of the wind, too."

"Well, it sure is a miracle they showed up when they did," Daphne sighs. "Those sea monsters could have sunk this ship."

Turn the page.

"I think the dolphins are food for the plesiosaurs and the plesiosaurs are food for the huracans," Danielle concludes. "We got caught in the middle of the food chain."

"I don't think it's over yet," Daphne warns and points to the sky. A flock of young huracans drift down and land on the ship. They plop onto the deck and perch in the rigging.

"They look exhausted!" Daphne observes.

"They've probably been flying since the destruction of Atlantis," Danielle says. "They've lost their habitat."

"We've got to help them!" Daphne says. She shouts to the passengers and crew: "The huracans saved this ship, now let's save their babies!"

Daphne leads the way by making a nest around several of the young pterosaurs. They curl up and fall asleep. The humans hurry to make more nests from ropes, sails and extra clothing.

"Prehistoric nursery school. I like it!" Danielle chuckles.

For the next few days, the adult huracans glide in the air above the refugee ship like guardians. The captain steers the ship in the direction the huracans fly and hopes they will lead him to land. Their babies stay on board and the humans take care of them.

One morning all the young huracans leave their nests and fly west. At the same time the ship's lookout shouts: "Land!"

Daphne and Danielle see the curve of a tropical island bay. "That looks ... familiar," Danielle says.

Suddenly Daphne and Danielle are back on Dr Jackson's diving boat. They are anchored in the exact same bay. "It's still here after all these centuries!" Danielle says.

"And so are we!" Daphne sighs with relief, but she can't help looking over the rail for a stray plesiosaur.

THE END

To follow another path, turn to page 11.

Shaggy and Scooby-Doo are given a choice between clear danger and certain doom. There's no good choice!

"How about a third choice? You let us go and we'll forget we saw you," Shaggy suggests.

"Reah," Scooby agrees.

"Into the cooking pot!" the king orders.

The natives lift the pole holding Shaggy and Scooby and march over to the cauldron with it. The rope is unwrapped, and the friends plop into the steaming liquid. **SPLOOOOSH!** They sink under the water but soon pop back up to the surface.

"Like, check it out, Scoobs! Our diving suits make us float!" Shaggy says. He turns onto his back and uses his flippers to swim around inside the kettle. Scooby doggie paddles in a big circle. The native king looks astonished.

"**SLUUURP!** Rhis is rummy!" Scooby says as he samples the broth in the pot.

Shaggy sips some of the simmering liquid.

"It needs a little salt," Shaggy suggests. "Where's the chef?"

One of the natives steps up. He wears a tall white head-dress that looks like a chef's hat.

"This recipe needs more veggies!" Shaggy says. "Carrots! Celery! Onions!"

The chef runs off. He returns with his arms loaded with vegetables. He tosses the veggies into the pot. Shaggy and Scooby swim around and around as fast as a blender. When they stop, the chef hands Shaggy a wooden spoon. Shaggy takes a taste of the soup.

"Perfect!" Shaggy declares.

The natives all clap with approval. The chef looks very happy. Even the king sips the soup and stops frowning.

SLUUUURP! SLUUUUURP! Suddenly all the soup disappears! The natives peek over the rim and see Shaggy and Scooby lying at the bottom of the cauldron. Their tummies are bulging!

Turn to page 75.

The mermaid queen swims through the water towards Fred and Velma. All the other mermaids back away as a sign of respect. Velma notices that the queen wears jewellery made from man-made objects and litter, but the other mermaids are dressed in seaweed and shells. They look like shabby peasants next to the splendid queen.

"You know that saying about one man's rubbish being another man's riches?" Velma says to Fred. "Well, she's wearing all of it."

The queen comes up to Fred and Velma and studies them closely.

"We must look as strange to her as she does to us," Fred says.

The queen pulls at their diving gear. She is curious about what Velma and Fred are wearing. The queen pulls on Fred's diving belt. When it doesn't loosen, she pulls harder and shakes Fred like a toy.

Turn the page.

"Give her your diving belt, Fred!" Velma shouts.

"I-I'm t-trying!" Fred stammers. He struggles to unsnap the belt. The queen shakes him so hard that he can't get a grip on the clip.

Velma takes off her diving belt and offers it to the mermaid. That seems to make the queen happy. She lets go of Fred and snatches the belt from Velma. The queen puts it around her neck like a necklace. The other mermaids make sounds of admiration.

"We'd better get out of here before she decides that she likes our air tanks or helmets," Velma suggests.

Fred and Velma slowly swim away as the queen and her subjects focus on the new prize. They don't get far.

"SHREEEEE!" the queen commands. The mermaids grab Fred and Velma.

"Too late. I think we're about to become a new line of jewellery," Fred gulps.

Turn to page 78.

Daphne swims over to the watery image of young Scooby.

"Scooby-Doo! Where are you?" Daphne asks. She reaches out and touches the wall of shimmering water. Suddenly her senses start to spin, and so does she. "Oh no, not another underwater tornado!"

Daphne shuts her eyes to avoid getting seasick. It doesn't really help. The spinning sensation stops as quickly as it started. Daphne opens her eyes and sees a terrifying sight!

A dinosaur looms over her. Its sharp teeth are only a few feet above her and a frightened Scooby pup.

"Yelp! Yelp! Help! Help!" the pup whimpers.

Daphne has to think fast! How is she going to fight off a hungry dino?

Finally she grabs her diving light and shines its powerful beam straight into the dinosaur's eye.

Turn the page.

The carnivore's pupil contracts rapidly. Next, Daphne grabs an emergency flare from her diving belt and lights it. She waves it in front of the bewildered beast. The heat, light and sound of the flare confuse the dinosaur even more. It stomps away to look for other prey.

"Hey, little guy, are you all right?" Daphne asks the cowering pup.

"Yipe! Yipe!" the pup shrieks and shrinks away from her.

"Oh! I'm still wearing my diving suit!" Daphne realizes. "That would scare me, too!"

Daphne pulls off her diving helmet and shakes out her beautiful red hair. The Scooby pup watches her with stars of adoration in his eyes. "Hi! My name is Daphne. What's yours?"

"Scaredy! Scaredy-Doo!" a voice shouts from behind Daphne and the pup.

Daphne turns and sees a pack of large dogs racing towards her. All of them look a lot like Scooby-Doo!

Turn to page 82.

"BUUUUURP!" Shaggy and Scooby belch. They ate all the soup in the cooking pot!

The native chef looks astonished. The natives look impressed. The king looks furious!

"Grab them!" the ruler orders.

"Ruh-roh!" Scooby cries.

Shaggy and Scooby try to run, but their flippers slip on the cooking pot. They can't get out! Scooby trips over Shaggy's floppy feet. The twosome tumble and fall against the side of the pot. **CLAAAANG!** Their weight tips the pot out of the fire pit. **RRRUUMBLE!** The pot starts to roll!

Shaggy and Scooby tumble inside the cauldron as it rolls like a bowling ball. It crashes through the village and into the jungle.

"*Yaaaa!*" Shaggy and Scooby yell.

The friends don't know where they're going. They have no control over the cauldron.

The giant iron pot rolls through the trees and bushes. No one can stop it, least of all Shaggy and Scooby-Doo!

Turn the page.

Suddenly the cauldron runs into a large hole. The pot spins around and around the hole, and when it stops, it's upside down. Shaggy and Scooby fall out of the pot and into the hole.

"*Yaaaa!*" they yell as they slide down a hidden mine shaft.

THUMP! CRAAAASH! Shaggy and Scooby land in the middle of a pile of wooden shipping crates.

"Ow!" Shaggy says as he picks splinters from his diving suit. Then he looks at what is inside the broken crates. "Wow!"

The crates are full of precious paintings and sculptures.

"This is an art-smuggling ring," Shaggy realizes.

"You meddling kids!" a voice shouts. Men in black uniforms run towards the friends.

Shaggy and Scooby flee! They duck into a room to hide, but someone is already there.

"Zoinks!" Shaggy yelps. Then he sees who it is. "Wait. Another king?"

"I'm the true king. I've been kidnapped!" the man says.

"That other guy is a fake!" Shaggy realizes as he unties the captive ruler.

Shaggy, Scooby and the king run towards the exit. Suddenly they meet up with the guards, the natives and the fake king all at the same time.

"Intruder! You have invaded my kingdom!" the true king says to the imposter. "You will face punishment!"

"Queen" Velma runs up to her friends as the warriors take the imposter away.

"I pretended to be the queen to find out where the real king was, but that fake king didn't give me a clue," Velma says. "Shaggy and Scooby, you solved the mystery!"

"Scooby-Dooby-Doo!" they cheer!

THE END

To follow another path, turn to page 11.

The mermaids grab Fred and Velma and stop them from leaving the cave. The queen snags the friends by their flippers and drags them into a deep hole in the cave wall. The hole leads to a chamber filled with stacks of man-made rubbish. Fred and Velma get added to one of the piles.

"Jinkies! I think we're in a treasure trove," Velma exclaims.

"Hey, I think I can use this stuff to escape!" Fred realizes.

"How?" Velma wonders.

"I have a plan," Fred proclaims and grabs bits and pieces from all the piles.

Velma watches in awe as Fred uses the objects to build a giant underwater robot!

"You have great mechanical skills, Fred, but I can't give you any points for style," Velma declares as she looks at the rubbish-tip robot.

Turn to page 80.

"Style isn't everything. Just don't repeat that to Daphne," Fred replies. "Let's get out of here!"

Fred and Velma climb into the hollow arms and legs of Fred's invention. They use their own limbs to make the robot move. Sort of.

"Velma! We need to walk forwards!" Fred says as he tries to move the legs.

"Okay, but I'm trying to keep our balance!" Velma replies as she holds out the arms.

The robot stumbles from the treasure trove like a zombie. It shambles into the main cave and into the colony of mermaids.

"YEEEE!" the mermaids shrill in fear. They hide behind their queen like a scared school of fish.

"SHREEEE!" the queen shrieks. She swims out of the cave as fast as she can.

The mermaids are left alone to face the underwater robot! They hug each other in fear.

"Don't worry, we aren't going to hurt you!" Velma says as she and Fred swim out of the robot.

Suddenly one of the mermaids swims up to Velma and hugs her! Then another mermaid hugs Fred. Soon all of the mermaids swarm around Fred and Velma and chatter like dolphins.

"I don't know their language, but I think they're happy," Velma guesses. "I think your recycled robot just freed them from a dictator."

"If you're right, that's got to be the best use of recycling ever!" Fred declares.

THE END

To follow another path, turn to page 11.

Daphne is surrounded by a pack of prehistoric dogs. They all look like Scooby-Doo!

The pup Daphne has just rescued runs to his mum. The leader of the pack faces the human stranger. "You're Scooby-Doo's ancestors!" Daphne realizes.

"I'm Yabba-Doo," the dog replies. "Who are you?"

"She said her name is Daphne! Can I keep her?" the pup pipes up. His mum sighs and rolls her eyes.

"We'll see. Let's go. That dinosaur might come back," Yabba declares.

The pack trots off and Daphne follows them back to a large cave. The rest of the family is there. A couple of teenage canines run up to the pup and tackle him.

"Ha! Ha! Scaredy can't hunt! All he came back with is his tail between his legs!" they tease.

"GRRR!" Daphne growls and pulls the bullies off the pup.

"I think the human is attached to you. You may keep her," Yabba-Doo tells Scaredy.

"Thanks, Dad! I'm going to call her Daphne-Doo!" Scaredy says. "Come on, Daphne, I'll show you my part of the cave!"

Daphne follows the pup to a small nook in the rock. The walls are covered with drawings and paintings of dinosaurs and the Doo family. "These are really good!" Daphne exclaims.

"No one has ever said that before, except Mum," the pup says. "Do you want to paint something?"

"Sure!" Daphne replies.

The pup pulls out a secret stash of charcoal and pigments. "I have to keep these hidden from everyone, especially my cousins."

Daphne watches the pup paint hunting scenes on the rock. She adds a few strokes of colour, but the art is all his.

"You're not a hunter, you're an artist!" Daphne exclaims proudly.

Turn to page 85.

"An artist always signs his work." Daphne dips his paw into paint and presses it onto the wall. "You're not Scaredy-Doo. You're Leonar-Doo."

"You're my best friend," the pup says and presses Daphne's handprint onto the wall, too.

The pup yawns and curls up in Daphne's lap. He goes to sleep, and soon Daphne does, too. *SLUUURP! SLUUURP!* No sooner does Daphne doze off than a wet tongue wakes her up! She looks around and sees that she's on the diving boat. Dr Jackson and her friends are there, and Scooby-Doo is licking her face.

"Scooby!" Daphne exclaims and hugs him. "I met your prehistoric ancestors!"

"Ruh? Ri have rancestors?" Scooby says.

"You sure do, and I helped save one from a dinosaur," Daphne declares.

"Rank rou," Scooby says. "Yabba-Dooby-Doo!"

THE END

To follow another path, turn to page 11.

The tribal king gives Shaggy and Scooby a choice of two fates.

"Hmmm... Which doom do I choose? Like, I don't know!" Shaggy says.

"If you can't decide, I'll decide for you!" the king declares. "Combat!"

The ruler gestures at the natives, and they untie Shaggy and Scooby from the pole. The rest of the villagers form a wide circle around the friends. One of the warriors steps into the circle and shakes a spear at Shaggy and Scooby.

"Ruh-roh!" Scooby gulps.

"Zoinks!" Shaggy shrieks.

The frightened friends start running in opposite directions inside the circle. The native warrior turns around and around, trying to decide which one to chase. He gets dizzy and falls over!

Another warrior steps into the ring. He picks up the spear the other warrior dropped and stomps towards Shaggy and Scooby-Doo.

Afraid but desperate, Shaggy and Scooby each strike a kung fu pose.

"Hee-yaa!" Shaggy screeches.

Shaggy and Scooby wave their arms around and chop at the air with their hands. The native warrior stands and stares at them. His face is covered with war paint, so it's hard to tell if he is impressed or confused – or both. At last Shaggy and Scooby get tired and fall to the ground.

The warrior strides towards the exhausted pair. Shaggy and Scooby are surprised when he walks straight past them.

"Get ready to run," he whispers to them.

The warrior suddenly grabs Queen Velma! He bursts through the circle of surprised villagers.

"Run!" he reminds Shaggy and Scooby.

The friends follow the fleeing warrior into the jungle. As soon as they catch up with him, they see that it's Fred in disguise.

Turn the page.

"Like, not that we aren't glad to see you, but how did you get here?" Shaggy asks.

"We were shot out of an underwater geyser," Fred replies.

"Hey! Ro were re!" Scooby says.

"Those natives found us, and the king took a liking to Velma," Fred explains. "I was trying to figure out a way to rescue her, and then you guys showed up."

"Where's Daphne?" Shaggy worries.

"Back at the geyser," Fred replies. "Now stop asking questions and save your breath for running!"

Turn to page 96.

The mermaids back away from Fred and Velma as the queen swims up to them. She is twice the size of the other mermaids and has different colouring. She looks like an orca, and her subjects look more like dolphins.

"Who knew there was more than one kind of mermaid?" Velma observes.

"Who knew there were mermaids in the first place?" Fred replies.

The queen glides up to Fred and Velma and pokes at their legs with her coral sceptre. Then she peers into their diving masks and stares at them eye-to-eye.

"Humans! Enemies!" the queen declares.

Fred and Velma are astonished.

"Hey! I heard her voice like it was inside my head!" Fred gasps.

"We're not enemies. We've only just met!" Velma protests.

"Hi! My name is Fred Jones, Jr, and this is my friend, Velma Dinkley," Fred introduces himself.

Turn the page.

"All humans are enemies. They are monsters who destroy our home," the queen proclaims.

"Uh, she's got us there, Velma. Humans do pollute and overfish the ocean," Fred agrees.

THOOOOM! Suddenly the whole cave shakes from an underwater shock wave! Bits of rock and coral drop from the ceiling. The mermaids squeal and twist their bodies in pain. **THOOOM!** Another shock wave hits, and then another.

"What is that?" Fred yelps.

"Humans," the mermaid queen replies.

"It's too strong to be sonar," Velma concludes. "But whatever it is, it's hurting them and ruining their cave."

"We've got to find out what's causing this. We've got to help the mermaids," Fred says.

"Use humans to fight humans? Good idea!" the queen decides.

The monarch squeals a high-pitched command to her subjects. The mermaids grab Fred and Velma.

The mermaids swim through a twisting maze of tunnels with their captives. They swim so quickly that Fred and Velma almost get seasick. At last they break through the surface of the water. There is a large ship nearby. **THOOOM! THOOOM!** Shock waves radiate from the ship.

"Well, now we know where the shock waves are coming from," Fred says.

"But we still don't know why," Velma replies. "Let's find out."

Fred and Velma swim towards the ship. The mermaids refuse to follow them. As soon as Velma gets close enough to the ship, she sees a string of large metal cylinders tied to the stern. One cylinder doesn't look like the rest.

"I know what this is, and it isn't good," Velma declares.

Turn to page 99.

Daphne can't resist reaching out and touching the image of Egyptian Scooby. Suddenly she feels dizzy. She shuts her eyes for a moment, and when she opens them she isn't in the underwater cave anymore. She is sitting on an Egyptian throne, dressed like a queen.

"Your Majesty, are you well? You almost fainted," a woman whispers in her ear.

"Your queen faints at the sight of her conquerors!" another voice proclaims. "You're doomed."

Daphne looks up and sees an Egyptian nobleman, but he has Scooby's head and face! He stands in front of the royal throne with his soldiers behind him. Daphne is surprised to see that they are wearing spacesuits!

"Surrender to Emperor Anubis, Ruler of the Sirius Star Empire!" Egyptian Scooby demands.

Daphne tries to make sense of what she's seeing, but what she's seeing doesn't make sense.

Turn the page.

"Sirius? That's the dog star," Daphne mutters to herself, trying to figure things out. "Okay, it makes sense that Anubis is from there. But why is Scooby on his side?"

When Queen Daphne does not reply to Egyptian Scooby, he raises his staff and rushes towards her throne.

"Do you surrender to Anubis?" Scooby shouts.

Everyone in the room gasps, but no one makes a move to stop the attack. Apart from Daphne. She uses her martial arts skills to block his blow. The crowd gasps again as Queen Daphne stands up from her throne and pushes Egyptian Scooby backwards.

"Yipe!" evil Scooby yelps as he lands on his tail.

No one moves, not even the space soldiers. Daphne has no idea what is going on here, so she bluffs. She stands over the fallen Scooby and gives him her best "furious" pose.

"I'm the queen, here. You've been a bad dog! Go to your room!" Daphne commands.

Egyptian Scooby looks confused. He was not expecting her to fight back.

"Now!" Daphne demands and stomps her foot.

Evil Scooby struggles to his feet. The space soldiers do not help him.

"You realize, of course, this means war," Scooby says as he slinks away. The space soldiers follow him out of the throne room.

The Egyptians cheer as soon as the enemy is gone. Daphne sits back down on the throne. Her knees feel weak.

"Jeepers, I just declared war on those alien invaders," Daphne gulps.

Queen Daphne does not get a chance to think about what just happened. Suddenly two of her Royal Guards grab her by the arms and lift her from her throne.

"Fred? Shaggy?" Daphne gasps. The guards look just like her two friends.

Turn to page 103.

The friends flee through the jungle. They can hear the angry native warriors chasing them. Fred carries Velma over his shoulder.

"You can put me down, Fred," Velma says.

"It's no trouble to carry you, Velma."

"No, I mean that this costume is pinching me! Put me down," Velma insists.

The gang halts, and Fred lowers Velma to the ground. She adjusts the royal clothing she is wearing and sees what is pinching her.

"It's this belt," Velma says. She takes it off. "Jinkies! This belt is a strand of raw diamonds!"

"Diamonds aren't mined in the Bahamas," Fred says.

"But I bet they're smuggled," Velma deduces.

"Uh, guys," Shaggy warns, "the natives are coming!"

"We have to run away to solve the diamond mystery another day," Velma says.

"Run!" Fred shouts.

The friends flee through the jungle. They don't stop until they find the geyser and Daphne! They run towards her as the angry natives burst out of the jungle.

"Re're roomed," Scooby whimpers as the warriors surround him and his friends.

"Get ready to dive," Fred whispers to the gang.

"Dive? Where?" Shaggy wonders.

"Dive there," Daphne says and nods towards the geyser shaft.

Shaggy and Scooby look down the empty hole. "Are you crazy?" Shaggy yelps.

Suddenly the ground rumbles under their feet. The geyser shoots up into the air. The natives back up in awe.

"Quick, put on your diving masks," Daphne says as the geyser starts to drop. "Now dive!"

The gang leaps into the geyser. The water level drops and carries them down into the hole. An underwater current catches them. Again, they are carried through a twisting tunnel.

Turn the page.

This time the friends are able to hold on to each other! They shoot out into a large cave.

"This is amazing!" Velma gasps at what she sees. "This is the Anubis temple. We're back where we started."

"Hi, kids, have you been exploring?" Dr Jackson asks.

"Sort of," Fred replies.

"Come and see my latest discovery!" Dr Jackson exclaims. They swim over to a painting on the underwater wall. The image shows a queen. Mystery Inc. gasps in surprise.

"Velma! That's you!" Fred says.

"And you're wearing the diamond belt!" Daphne exclaims.

"I guess we have more than one mystery on our hands," Velma concludes.

THE END

To follow another path, turn to page II.

Fred and Velma hide under the stern of the ship and study the cylinders on the tow-line.

"This is an echo-sounding array," Velma says. "It sends out a sound pulse like sonar but much, much stronger. The mermaids are sensitive to it, just like dolphins and whales."

"But what's it being used for and who is using it?" Fred wonders.

"I can't see any identification on the ship, which means it's probably illegal," Velma concludes.

"Whatever these people are doing, we have to stop them," Fred says. "I have a plan! Follow me."

Fred dives under the surface. Velma follows him to the line of cylinders. The array is silent for now. Fred grabs one of the cylinders and hauls it towards the ship's propeller. Velma sees what he is doing and helps him tangle the tow-line and cylinders around the propeller.

Turn the page.

"The next time they try to use the array they'll give their ship a sonic screech!" Fred says.

"And they won't be able to go anywhere before I call the Marine Police," Velma promises.

Suddenly mermaids zoom past Fred and Velma like a swift pod of dolphins. They shriek and squeal at a high pitch. Fred and Velma clap their hands to their helmets, trying to block out the sound.

"Are they happy or angry?" Velma wonders.

Fred can barely hear her over the helmet radio.

"I don't know, but they sure are loud!" Fred replies.

Fred and Velma swim to the surface, but the noise is almost as loud as it is under water. They see the ship's crew running around on the deck in a panic!

"It's the curse! These waters are haunted!" one of the crew yells.

Turn to page 102.

The ship's engines start to rumble. Then they stop dead. The tangled tow-line has done its job.

"It's the curse of Atlantis! We're doomed!" one of the crew wails.

"Don't be stupid! I made that up!" the captain shouts. Then his eyes widen in fear.

The orca queen rises out of the water and stands on her tail. **SHREEEEE!** The mermaid shrieks at the captain and crew like a sea ghost. Then she disappears under the waves.

Fred and Velma meet up with the queen and her subjects to say goodbye. "We'll make sure those bad humans are punished," Fred promises.

"Good humans," the queen proclaims and pats Fred and Velma on their heads. Then she and her subjects disappear beneath the water.

"It's going to be a long swim back to the diving boat." Velma sighs.

THE END

To follow another path, turn to page 11.

The guards don't speak. They take Daphne from the throne room and lead her to two women in royal Egyptian garb. Daphne is glad when she sees who it is.

"Velma! Danielle!" Daphne cries with relief. "What's going on?"

"Who is Velma? I am your sister, Vel'ma'at," Velma replies.

"And I am Daan'a'el," Danielle adds.

"Um, sorry. I got confused," Daphne stammers. "What's happening?"

"Anubis wants to invade Egypt, and only you can stop him," Vel'ma'at says.

"How?" Daphne asks.

"This way," Daan'a'el replies. She guides Daphne through a secret door in the palace wall. They go down a steep, spiral staircase to an underground crypt. A huge stone coffin sits in the middle of the chamber.

"Open the Tomb of the Ancients and save Egypt!" Vel'ma'at pleads Daphne.

Turn the page.

Daphne runs her hands around the coffin but can't find a seam or trigger to open it. She turns towards Daan'a'el and Vel'ma'at and shrugs.

"We're doomed," Daphne says. Suddenly the coffin opens. "Oh! The sound of my voice must have done it!"

Inside is a jade mask. As soon as Daphne picks it up it attaches to her face! Armour forms over her body!

"I hope this is a good thing," Daphne says.

"Aha! You've led me to the secret tomb!" evil Scooby proclaims as he enters the chamber. "Now Emperor Anubis will have the Armour of Atlantis!"

ZAAAAP! An energy beam from the armour hits evil Scooby, and he collapses.

"You forgot that I'm already wearing the armour," Daphne points out.

"My brilliant plan is ruined!" Egyptian Scooby wails. He rips off his dog-head mask to reveal a human face underneath.

"Ramses!" Vel'ma'at and Daan'a'el gasp.

"I wanted to be Pharaoh, and I would have gotten away with it, too," Ramses complains.

"Except that I found the Atlantis Armour first," Daphne says. "Now I can use it to defeat Anubis!"

* * *

A few days later, Queen Daphne stands on the beach of a faraway tropical island. She places the jade mask in a small temple guarded by a statue of Anubis.

"Let this be a monument to the defeat of Anubis!" Queen Daphne declares as she seals the temple. "The Armour of Atlantis will be safe here. I have a feeling it won't be discovered for centuries."

THE END

To follow another path, turn to page 11.

AUTHOR

Laurie S. Sutton has been reading comics since she was a child. She grew up to become an editor for Marvel, DC Comics, Starblaze and Tekno Comics. She has written Adam Strange for DC, Star Trek: Voyager for Marvel, plus Star Trek: Deep Space Nine and Witch Hunter for Malibu Comics. There are long boxes of comics in her wardrobe where there should be clothing and shoes. Laurie has lived all over the world. She currently lives in Florida, USA.

ILLUSTRATOR

Scott Neely has been a professional illustrator and designer for many years. Since 1999, he's been an official Scooby-Doo and Cartoon Network artist, working on characters such as those from Dexter's Laboratory, Johnny Bravo, Courage the Cowardly Dog, Powerpuff Girls and more. He has also worked on Pokémon, Mickey Mouse Clubhouse, My Friends Tigger & Pooh, Handy Manny, Strawberry Shortcake, Bratz and many other popular characters. He lives near Philadelphia, USA, and has a scrappy Yorkshire Terrier called Alfie.

GLOSSARY

Anubis god of tombs and weigher of the hearts of the dead; represented as having the head of a jackal

artifacts objects made or changed by human beings, especially those used in the past

Atlantis legendary island said to have existed in the Atlantic Ocean west of Gibraltar and to have sunk beneath the sea

conquerors people who defeat and take control of an enemy

corrosion process of being destroyed or eaten away bit by bit

dictator someone who has complete control of a country, often ruling it unjustly

genetic related to the study of genes and how human characteristics are passed on

Mayans related to a group of ancient American Indian tribes that lived in southern Mexico and Central America

mutant living thing that has developed different characteristics because of a change in its parents' genes

Neanderthals primate mammals that belong to the same family as human beings; lived from about 30,000 to 200,000 years ago

YOU CHOOSE JOKES!

YOU CHOOSE which punchline is funniest!

Why did the mermaid check out a book from the library?
a. Have you ever seen a mermaid without a "tale"?
b. She was hungry for bookworms.
c. She was "fin-ished" with her old book.

What did the boy eel say to the girl eel?
a. "I get a charge out of you!"
b. "You light up my life!"
c. "I can tell I'm in love – it's 'a moray'!"

What kind of seafood does Scooby like to eat?
a. Octo-pie.
b. Sole-food.
c. Any kind. If he can SEE food, he'll eat it!

Velma: I heard the goldfish restaurant has closed.

a. **Fred:** "Yeah, it tanked."
b. **Daphne:** "It went belly-up."
c. **Shaggy:** "And the clown fish said the food tasted funny!"

How can you communicate with someone when they're under water?

a. Easy – drop them a line!
b. Wear a "herring" aid!
c. Use your shell phone!

Why did the dolphin steal Shaggy's lunch from the beach?

a. The dolphin likes all the "sand which is" there!
b. Because it shore looked tasty!
c. I don't know, but he did it on porpoise.

LOOK FOR MORE...

← YOU CHOOSE STORIES →

THE CHOICE IS YOURS!